This **Rising Moon** book belongs to

To Max, Juliana, Amelia, and Carmen
—S.L.

To my folks,
Skit and Jim—creativity and heart
—B.M.

Josefina Javelina

A Hairy Tale

by Susan Lowell

Illustrated by
Bruce MacPherson

rising moon

ONCE UPON A TIME, way out in the desert, there were three little javelinas, and their names were Juan, José, and Josefina (Ho-seh-FEE-na).

Javelinas (ha-ve-LEE-nas) are hairy, hoggy critters, wild and free. They love to eat cactus—thorns and all.

From dusk to dawn, Juan and José gobbled and crunched.

"S-s-sweet!" they slurped.

"Snur-r-rp!" they burped.

Then they scratched each other's backs and snoozed all day.

But their sister was different.

Josefina was a dreamer. With her head in the clouds and stars in her eyes, she sang and danced wherever she went:

> *"Oh, I can play the concertina,*
>> *And I wish I were a ballerina!"*

"Snorg!" said her brothers.

But Josefina longed for excitement. "Ah, to be famous! My name in lights! My hooves on point! My fur in tights!"

When the big red sun went down, and the bats began
to fly, the three little javelinas trotted off to their local
watering hole.

At the Oasis Snack Bar and Cantina, Juan and José
liked to rock and roll. Crickets fiddled and toads
croaked. Bunnies hip-hopped. Bobcats bebopped.

Far away in the desert darkness, Coyote howled
at the moon.

Meanwhile, handsome Julio and the Javelina Heartstrings played a warm and spicy salsa tune.

"**Boom-boom chile boom!**" sang Julio.

"*You make my snout sing!*

My hair is smoking! My heart goes zing!

Boom-boom chile BOOM!"

Nibbling on a prickly pear, Josefina hummed to herself, "The Oasis Snack Bar and Cantina has no place for a ballerina!"

Great Horned Owl winked at her and whispered, "Doooooo something new!"

And the very next day, something wonderful came by snail.

"A card!" said Josefina. "From my cousin Angelina, way out west in Pasadena…"

"California is cool-issimo!" wrote Angelina. "Wish you were here!"

Josefina did three pirouettes and a giant leap.

"Pasadena!" she cried. "That's right next door to **HOLLYWOOD**!"

And she burst out singing:

"Let me go where the grass is greener!
I'll pack my tutu and concertina
And hit the road to Pasadena!"

The road was long; the road was rough…

"Yikes!" cried Josefina. "Traffic!"

But at last she got to Pasadena.

"Fun-a-rama!" said Angelina. "It's my cousin Josefina!"

And Josefina began to dance and sing.

"*I can play the concertina,*
And I WILL become a ballerina!"

"Fabu-lissimo!" said Angelina. "Let's go!"

At the Big Break Talent Agency, Josefina did her act for a dude in a fancy suit.

The sign on the door read:

WHITE E. LAMB
A Taste for Talent • A Nose for the Stars

"Wild! Totally wild!" cheered Mr. Lamb. "Baby, you're a javelina superstar! Like Gregory Peccary and Cary Grunt!"

"But I sing," said Josefina.

"Yes! Like Frank Swineatra!" cried Mr. Lamb. "And Elvis Bristly!"

"And she dances," said Angelina. "And she plays—"

"Strong… yet tender," he sighed. "Scrrrumptious! Just like Hairilyn Monroe!"

"HE reminds ME of somebody, too," thought Josefina. "But who?"

"Come back tomorrow, girls," grinned Mr. Lamb. He yodeled a little song:

"It's your debut,
My sweetie-poo!
Ow-woo!"

"**Super-mega-tastic!**" shouted Angelina. But Josefina worried all night long. "Should lambs have fangs?" she wondered.

And suddenly she was homesick. She missed her hairy brothers, Juan and José, and she was hungry for a prickly pear.

"Slump-a-rama!" cried Angelina.

"I can't go on," moaned Josefina.

"But-but-ballerinas can't stay home and DUST!" gasped Angelina.

Finally, slowly, Josefina smiled and sang:

"No, I didn't come to Pasadena
To sing and dance with a vacuum cleaner!"

Early the next morning, back at the talent agency, Josefina fluffed up her tutu and tied on her toe shoes. Mr. Lamb's shadow loomed behind his window. But something about him was strangely different… and so was the sign on the door.

R. BEN COYOTE
Prankster • Predator

"Bum-issimo!" screamed Angelina.

And off they ran through the streets of Pasadena, with Coyote hot on their heels.

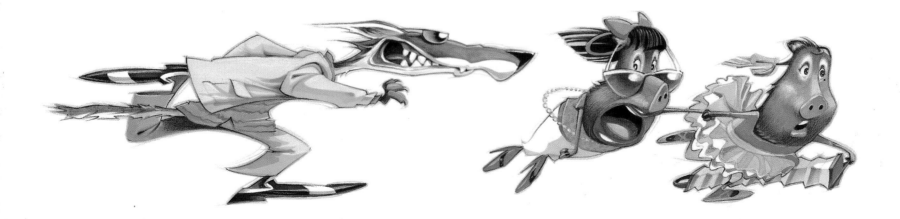

"Yikes!" cried Josefina. "Traffic!"

Horses pranced. Princesses waved. Tubas honked and cymbals smashed. Three giant pigs floated slowly down the street. It was a parade! But who was hiding behind the Three Pigs?

"LOOK OUT!" cried Angelina.

KKKRRRIP! Coyote ate a big bite of Josefina's tutu.

"Run, Angelina!" she shouted, and Angelina escaped.

Then Josefina spun like a top, leaped like a lizard, and flew like a shooting star. Huffing and puffing, Coyote fell behind.

All across the nation, people watched on TV. "What grace!" they said. "What footwork!" Josefina waltzed past the Tortoise and the Hare. She danced circles around Cinderella.

"What a ballerina!" people said. "She's another Anna Piglova. She jumps like the great Boaryshnikov! She's a PRIMA JAVELINA BALLERINA!"

Coyote sneaked by the Three Bears and hid behind
Red Riding Hood. Whisk! SNAP!

But Josefina put some dip in her hip and some slide
in her glide. She showed Coyote six high kicks, and she
made him do the splits. Then she joined a marching
band and played her concertina while everybody sang:

"Never bite a ballerina!

Nothing in the whole wide world is meaner

Than a bitten ballerina!"

Behind their backs, Coyote vanished in a cloud of smog.

When the parade was over, the phone began to ring. Josefina was famous! And soon she left her mark on Hollywood. In the *Nutcracker*, she starred as the Sugar Plum Hairy.

But…even though she was a prima ballerina, Josefina was terribly homesick. She missed the hot desert sun and the cool desert moon. She missed the Oasis Snack Bar and Cantina. She even missed Juan's snorts and José's burps. And she was starving for a prickly pear!

But then came the very best call of all. "Josefina, this is Julio," said a voice from the past. "Would you—could you—ever do a show at the Oasis Snack Bar and Cantina?"

The moon shone like a spotlight on the desert watering hole. It was full to the brim, and the prickly pears were ripe. What a party! Even the skunks, snakes, centipedes, and scorpions were welcome.

"Snarf! Slupp!" said Juan and José.
"Yum-yum-issimo!" said Angelina.
The Javelina Heartstrings played, and
Josefina danced like lightning in the
summer night. She did something new!
"Dreams do come true!" she cooed.
"Boom-boom chile boom!" sang Julio.
*"The Oasis Snack Bar and Cantina
Loves you, SALSA BALLERINA!*
Boom-boom chile BOOM!"
"¡Olé!" cried Josefina Javelina.

And way off in the distance,

Coyote sang the blues.

www.risingmoonbooks.com

Composed in the United States of America
Printed in China

Edited by Theresa Howell
Designed by Katie Jennings

FIRST IMPRESSION 2005
Hardcover ISBN 0-87358-790-1
Softcover ISBN 0-87358-895-9

05 06 07 08 09   5 4 3 2 1

Library of Congress Cataloging-in-Publication Data

Lowell, Susan, 1950-
Josefina javelina : a hairy tale / by Susan Lowell ; illustrated by Bruce MacPherson.
p. cm.
Summary: Josefina, a javelina who dreams of becoming a famous ballerina,
heads for California hoping to be discovered,
but her cousin Angelina takes her to a talent agent who looks strangely familiar.
[1. Pigs—Fiction. 2. Coyote—Fiction. 3. Ballet dancing—Fiction. 4. Homesickness—Fiction.
5. Hollywood (Los Angeles, Calif.)—Fiction. 6. Southwest, New—Fiction.] I. MacPherson, Bruce, W. 1960- ill. II. Title.
PZ7.L9648Jo 2005
[E]—dc22
2004028873